Ripley's Believe It or Not!

Developed and produced by Ripley Publishing Ltd

This edition published and distributed by:

Mason Crest
450 Parkway Drive, Suite D, Broomall, PA 19008
www.masoncrest.com

Copyright © 2010 by Ripley Entertainment Inc. This edition printed in 2013.
All rights reserved. Ripley's, Believe It or Not!, and Ripley's Believe It or Not! are registered trademarks of Ripley Entertainment Inc. No part of this publication may be reproduced in whole or in part, or stored in a retrieval system, or transmitted in any form or by any means, electronic, mechanical, photocopying, recording, or otherwise, without written permission from the publishers. For information regarding permission, write to VP Intellectual Property, Ripley Entertainment Inc., Suite 188, 7576 Kingspointe Parkway, Orlando, Florida, 32819
website: ripleybooks.com

Printed and bound in the United States of America

First printing
9 8 7 6 5 4 3 2 1

Ripley's Believe It or Not!
Extraordinary Feats
ISBN: 978-1-4222-2779-4 (hardback)
ISBN: 978-1-4222-2796-1 (paperback)
ISBN: 978-1-4222-9040-8 (e-book)
Ripley's Believe It or Not!—Complete 8 Title Series
ISBN: 978-1-4222-2769-5

Cataloging-in-Publication Data on file with the Library of Congress

PUBLISHER'S NOTE
While every effort has been made to verify the accuracy of the entries in this book, the Publisher's cannot be held responsible for any errors contained in the work. They would be glad to receive any information from readers.

WARNING
Some of the stunts and activities in this book are undertaken by experts and should not be attempted by anyone without adequate training and supervision.

EXTRAORDINARY FEATS

www.MasonCrest.com

EXTRAORDINARY FEATS

Outrageous accomplishments. Open your eyes to the most spectacular stunts and incredible exploits from around the world. Discover the extreme Niagara Falls daredevils, the truckers that risk their lives driving on long ice roads, and the motorbike that looks like a decaying corpse!

The Scubacraft is a boat and a submarine that can dive underwater to depths of nearly 100 ft (30 m)...

AMAZON MARATHON

British ex-army officer Ed Stafford began the trip of his life in April 2008, when he set out to walk the entire length of the Amazon River in South America, from its source to the Atlantic Ocean. He hopes to become the first man ever to do this and to highlight rainforest deforestation in the process. The river is 4,000 mi (6,400 km) long, but Ed thinks he will have walked almost 6,000 mi (9,650 km) by the time he is finished because the river is so wide and deep in so many places that he can't always take the shortest route. By February 2010, Ed had passed the halfway point of his 4,000-mi (6,400-km) trek, accompanied by a local guide, Cho, and with much of his "walk" spent chest deep in murky water. Hiking through one of the wildest environments on Earth, Ed has faced venomous snakes, flooding, electric eels, piranhas, and jaguars. He has been pursued by armed Peruvian tribespeople and been wrongly arrested on suspicion of murder. Traveling light with only a backpack, he is also at risk of scurvy or even starvation, often forced to forage in the jungle and catch piranhas for breakfast.

Preparing for the day

"Every morning I wake with the sun. I click my stiff neck from side to side and reach for my malaria tablets. These get swigged down with iodinated water that is hanging in a bottle above my head.

As we are usually in the middle of nowhere, I roll out of my hammock without any kit on. I slip into my Crocs to stumble to my washing line. Cho, my guide, and I live with just two sets of clothes—one for the day that is usually gritty and wet, and one for the evening that is always clean and dry. The wet clothes don't dry on the line overnight as the humidity is high and the airflow stifled by the thick trees. The line is there more to keep the clothes off the wet ground. I put them on without too much thinking and I hardly notice throughout the day that they are wet. On go my socks (with holes in them) and my jungle boots. It's now five past seven and I wander over to the fire area while brushing my teeth.

Usually the wood is wet, as neither Cho nor I have the ability to collect wood for the following morning and try to dry it. This is part laziness, part cockiness that we don't need to. One of us heads off with our machete and looks for dead wood that is hanging in the trees. Dead wood found on the floor is too wet. I snap a twig to make sure it is dead enough: if the wood bends beyond 90 degrees, and doesn't break cleanly in two, then it's too green and won't burn.

Once back at the fire area we make a small platform of logs, and light a piece of tree resin that will act as tinder and burn for ages. I then either add small twigs or shavings from the inside of large logs that are wet on the outside—but nice and dry inside. Usually we have water on the boil by half past seven.

Breakfast is always white rice and sometimes we get a reasonable catch of river fish and we don't need to open a can of tuna. The job of collecting the fishing net from the river is unpopular because the water is cold at this time in the morning and you have to swim to retrieve it. Removing a piranha from the net requires certain caution as, although their reputation as maneaters is largely unfounded, they do have very sharp teeth. The fish are usually catfish, trout, and piranha and they get gutted and barbecued while the rice is cooking.

Concurrently, Cho and I nip back to our hammocks and pack everything away. Everything goes into a huge rubber sack that sits inside our backpacks—that way it's all 100 percent waterproof and we can swim with our packs on our backs and know that the Macbook and sat phone are fine.

We make enough rice to put half in our Tupperware boxes and save it for lunchtime. By the time we've finished eating breakfast, we are normally ready and packed. Between 8 and 8.30, we haul the 32–35-kg packs onto our mosquito-bitten backs and we are on the move once more."

www.ripleybooks.com

TOMATO FORCE

In Guiyang, China in 2009, hundreds of people hurled tomatoes at each other at a bizarre promotional event organized by a local shopping center. Inspired by the famous Tomatina festival in Spain, the juicy battle required a massive haul of tomatoes weighing more than 20 family cars and costing almost $15,000.

RIB FEAST
Pat "Deep Dish" Bertoletti of Chicago, Illinois, ate 5 lb 12 oz (2.6 kg) of ribs in 12 minutes at the Best in the West Nugget World Rib Eating Championship in Sparks, Nevada, in September 2009.

DREAM DRIVE
Graham and Eirene Naismith of London, England, sold their house, gave away their furniture, and spent ten months driving 31,116 mi (50,076 km) all the way to Australia and then around the entire circumference of the country—with three children under eight. Driving a Toyota Land Cruiser, they traveled through 19 countries and crossed three continents.

DINOSAUR CAFÉ
At the T-Rex Café in Kansas City, Kansas, customers can eat with dinosaurs. The diner's prehistoric environment features life-size animatronic dinosaurs and bubbling geysers, and the chance to dig up dinosaur fossils.

MASS CRUNCH
More than 39,000 baseball fans ate potato chips simultaneously in the middle of the second inning of a game between the New York Mets and the Cincinnati Reds at Citi Field, New York, in July 2009. The crunch could be heard all over the ballpark.

ROBOT CHEFS
A restaurant in China serves meals cooked by robot chefs. Hundreds of recipes for traditional Chinese dishes have been stored in the databases of the computers that control the movements of the two robots at the I Robot restaurant in Nanning, Guangxi Province. Human involvement is limited to preparing the ingredients.

GIANT DOG
More than 2,000 people ate a 660-ft-long (200-m) hot dog in Santa Marta, Colombia. Twelve of the city's leading fast-food cooks used 220 lb (100 kg) of bread, 275 lb (125 kg) of sausages, 250 bottles of sauce, and tons of vegetables and cheese to make the dog.

MODEL FLOTILLA
In the course of 75 years, Peter Tamm of Hamburg, Germany, has amassed a collection of 36,000 model ships (each built to 1:1,250 scale), thousands of photographs of ships, a maritime library of more than 100,000 volumes, and 15,000 ship menus, some dating back to the 1890s.

MINCE DISH
The town of Ehden, Lebanon, produced a giant circular kibbeh—a dish of minced meat and cracked wheat—that covered an area of 215 sq ft (20 sq m). The dish required 265 lb (120 kg) of mince, 21 gal (80 l) of olive oil, 175 lb (80 kg) of cracked wheat, 11 lb (5 kg) of salt, and 2 lb (1 kg) of pepper.

HEROIC REPAIR
In July 2009, after an airplane due to fly from Menorca, Spain, to Glasgow, Scotland, developed an engineering fault, vacationers were spared an eight-hour delay when one of the passengers fixed the plane himself.

Holy Cannoli

Speed eater Kevin Basso devoured 17 whole cannoli at the 2009 Little Italy Cannoli Eating Competition in New York City. Kevin finished third, with winner "Crazy Legs" Conti gulping down 20½ of the traditional Italian dessert pastries in just six minutes.

Ripley's Believe It or Not! | **EXTRAORDINARY FEATS**

SNOW BRAKES

Extreme driver and keen snowboarder Ken Block drove his $150,000 Subaru rally car up onto the slopes at Snowpark, New Zealand, in 2007. After towing several snowboarders around the course at high speed, Californian Block raced professional boarder Torstein Horgmo down a 55-ft (16.8-m) ramp, soaring 70 ft (21 m) over the snow and landing cleanly on the other side.

Versatile Craft

Welsh engineers have created a boat that can operate above or below the waves. Above water, the Scubacraft is propelled by a 160-horsepower engine; when submerged, it is powered by electric thrusters and can descend to a depth of nearly 100 ft (30 m). As it is not a pressurized submarine, those on board must wear scuba-diving gear when diving below the water.

RAIL FEARS
British railway pioneer George Stephenson (1781–1848) told public officials that trains would never go faster than 12 mph (19 km/h). This was to allay public fears that speeds of over 12 mph would bring about mental disorders among passengers.

BUS RESCUE
When the driver of a New York City school bus full of children suffered a fatal heart attack while at the wheel, 16-year-old Rachel Guzy took control and brought the vehicle to a halt as it sped toward a busy intersection. Driver Ramon Fernandez collapsed and tumbled out of the moving bus, but Rachel, who does not know how to drive, jumped into his seat and pulled the emergency brake, slowing the bus right down before it gently crashed into a van.

MISSING TRACK
Driving his train along the track in Hungary's Somogy County, Farkas Kolos suddenly realized that the track ahead had completely disappeared. He slammed on the brakes and managed to bring the train to a halt just short of where the track ended. Police confirmed that 2 mi (3.2 km) of track had been stolen.

LOST CAR RESURFACES
A car that had been buried beneath the dangerous mudflats of Brean Beach, Somerset, England, for 36 years suddenly resurfaced in 2009. Terry Hart's Vauxhall Victor sank in the mud in 1973 after he was trapped by the swift incoming tide. Rough weather and choppy seas eventually led to the car's heavily corroded remains being uncovered.

STEAM POWER
A steam car reached an average speed of 139.8 mph (225 km/h) on two runs over a distance of a mile at the Edwards Air Force Base, California, in August 2009—the fastest speed recorded by a steam car in 103 years! The 25-ft-long (7.6-m) British-built car, driven by Charles Burnett III, actually touched 151 mph (243 km/h) on its second run and has been dubbed "the fastest kettle in the world."

FLYING CAR
From 1949 to 1960, Longview, Washington State, engineer Moulton Taylor built six cars that could also fly. His prototype Aerocar had folding wings that allowed the car to be converted into a plane in five minutes by one person. It could drive at 60 mph (96 km/h) and fly at 110 mph (180 km/h).

CORVETTE BURIAL
In 1994, George Swanson of Hempfield, Pennsylvania, was buried in his beloved 1984 Corvette car. His cremated remains still sit in the driver's seat of the Corvette, which is buried in the local cemetery where it occupies 12 contiguous plots.

CYCLING TOUR
Over a period of nine years, Keiichi Iwasaki from Maebashi, Japan, has cycled more than 28,000 mi (45,000 km) through 37 countries. He originally set out on his Raleigh Shopper bicycle in 2001 to tour Japan, but enjoyed himself so much that he caught a ferry to South Korea and has not returned home since.

WRONG SYDNEY
When Dutchman Joannes Rutten and his 15-year-old grandson Nick booked a flight to Sydney, Australia, in 2009, a mix-up caused them to end up in the small former mining town of Sydney, Nova Scotia, Canada. They set off from Amsterdam hoping to visit relatives in Australia, only to touch down on Cape Breton Island, 10,000 mi (16,000 km) from their intended destination.

LONG BIKE
Colin Furze of Lincolnshire, England, spent two months creating a 46-ft-long (14-m) motorbike. He used two Honda 50cc mopeds, which he extended with pieces of aluminum. The elongated bike can travel at speeds of up to 30 mph (48 km/h) but needs six widths of an ordinary road to turn!

12 Ripley's Believe It or Not! | EXTRAORDINARY FEATS

PLANE CRAZY

In perhaps the greatest feat of strength ever, Rev. Kevin Fast from Cobourg, Ontario, Canada, successfully pulled a giant Globemaster airplane weighing 416,000 lb (188,694 kg)—the weight of more than 50 African elephants—for 29 ft (8.8 m) across the runway at an airbase in Trenton, Canada, in 2009.

ℝ PIGEON SERVICE

A carrier pigeon in South Africa proved faster at delivering data than broadband Internet. The pigeon took 1 hour 8 minutes to fly the 50 mi (80 km) from Pietermaritzburg to Durban with a data card strapped to its leg—and including download, the transfer took just over two hours. In that time only four percent of the data had been transferred using the country's leading Internet service provider.

ℝ UNCHANGED UNDERPANTS

Despite being huddled together on the International Space Station with as many as 12 colleagues, Japanese astronaut Koichi Wakata wore the same underpants for a month—and nobody complained. Called J-ware, the type of odorless underwear he was wearing has been developed by Japanese scientists and is designed to kill bacteria, absorb water, insulate the body, and dry quickly.

NAVAL STUDY
To discover how lint accumulates in the human navel, Dr. Georg Steinhauser of the Vienna University of Technology in Austria spent three years studying 503 pieces of fluff from his own belly button. He concluded that there is a particular type of body hair that traps pieces of stray lint and draws them in.

BULLET PROOF
An Icelandic inventor has designed a breast pocket handkerchief that can stop a bullet. Sruli Recht has created a handkerchief made from Kevlar, which is five times stronger than steel and can withstand temperatures of 750°F (400°C).

LASER BLAST
British scientists have made a transparent form of aluminum by bombarding the metal with a laser producing brief pulses of X-ray light. Each pulse is more powerful than the output of a power plant supplying electricity to an entire city.

TRICKY PROBLEM
Capable of 200 trillion calculations per second, a computer network in Jülich, Germany, spent more than a year computing the answer to a single physics question.

BIKE JUMP
In Chicago, Illinois, in July 2009, U.S. freestyle motocross star Ronnie Renner launched into a jump that took him more than 63 ft (19 m) above the ground. Riding his motorbike up a 22-ft-high (6.7-m) quarterpipe, he soared 41 ft 5 in (12.6 m) into the air upside down before landing on a ramp, giving him a total height of 63 ft 5 in (19.33 m).

PEDAL POWER
Sam Whittingham of British Columbia, Canada, can reach a speed of over 82 mph (132 km/h)—without an engine. Relying solely on human power, his recumbent bicycle clocked a speed of 82.4 mph (132.6 km/h) on a flat section of road at Battle Mountain, Nevada, in 2009.

HIGH ROLLER
Branden Moyen of Shillington, Pennsylvania, has built a model of a roller coaster 36 ft (11 m) tall and 50 ft (15 m) long from around 40,000 pieces of the construction toy K'NEX. The track measures about 400 ft (122 m) in length and the roller-coaster car travels at speeds up to 70 mph (115 km/h) after being slingshotted to the top of the first hill by 25 rubber bands. His model is a 1:10-scale replica of Klinga Da, a giant steel roller coaster at Six Flags Great Adventure, New Jersey.

CENTENARY JUMP
Peggy McAlpine from Stirling, Scotland, celebrated her 100th birthday, in October 2007, by paragliding from the top of a mountain range in Cyprus. Peggy, who is partially sighted and has lived through the reign of five British monarchs and more than 25 prime ministers, leaped from a 2,500-ft (760-m) peak in northern Cyprus for a 15-minute tandem flight.

EAR ACHE

Rakesh Sharma from India strains as he lifts 105 lb (48 kg) with his ears in Punjab, India, in October 2009. He attaches straps and a wooden clamp to his ears before slowly lifting the weights from the ground.

14 Ripley's Believe It or Not! | EXTRAORDINARY FEATS

Low Flyer

This peculiar contraption, photographed in 1922, is one of the earliest helicopters. Spaniard Raul Pescara's machine used four sets of blades, rather than the single blades used on modern helicopters. Unfortunately, his invention managed to get only 5 ft (1.5 m) off the ground.

Bent Barrel

In 1953, an M3 submachine gun was manufactured with a barrel that curved at right angles. It was designed for shooting over obstacles and around corners!

Bag of Tricks

In 1963, John H.T. Rinfret came up with an unusual invention to foil opportunistic robberies. His anti-bandit bag could be instantly pulled open with a chain, spilling all the contents onto the ground.

...MAD INVENTIONS...MAD INVENTIONS...MAD I

Ice Ride

The famous Ford Model T car was converted into an early version of the snowmobile in 1937. The vehicle had caterpillar belts around the regular rear tires, and metal skis were used in place of the front wheels. Such modified classics could reach around 18 mph (29 km/h) in thick snow.

Visionary

Science-fiction author Hugo Gernsback was way ahead of his time when he invented these television glasses, for portable TV viewing, which he unveiled in 1963.

...MAD INVENTIONS...MAD INVENTIONS...

www.ripleybooks.com

TASTY DE-LIGHT

Constructed by California-based artist Ya Ya Chou, this amazing gummy bear chandelier is made entirely from the famous candy bears and can remain fresh and on display for up to two years! Formed by stringing hundreds of different flavored gummies together with beads and string, the chandelier is just one of the pieces in a series of gummy-bear sculptures, which also include a bearskin rug and a deer.

PERFECT CHEESE
With the help of scientists from England's Bristol University, West Country Farmhouse Cheesemakers have devised what they claim is the mathematical formula for the perfect cheese sandwich. The formula contains nine algebraic variables, covering such essentials as the thickness of the Cheddar cheese, the thickness of the bread, the dough flavor modifier, the amount of mayonnaise, the thickness of tomato, and the depth of pickle.

NUGGET DROP
To welcome in the New Year in 2009, a chicken restaurant in McDonough, Georgia, dropped a plaster chicken nugget 6 ft 6 in (2 m) tall and weighing 795 lb (360 kg) into a giant vat of fake dipping sauce.

EXPENSIVE TASTE
Gennaro Pelliccia, a London-based Italian coffee taster with more than 18 years of experience, has had his tongue insured for nearly $14 million. His job is to test every batch of raw beans before they leave the firm's roastery and he is banned from eating curry within two days of tasting sessions in case the spices dull his sensitivity.

CHOCOLATE LOVER
Peggy Griffiths from Devon, England, eats 30 bars of chocolate a week—and in 2009 she celebrated her 100th birthday. She has eaten an estimated 70,000 Cadbury's Dairy Milk bars in her lifetime, amounting to an incredible 4 tons of chocolate. Chocoholic Peggy used to run a candy store in the 1930s, but it closed down because she ate all the profits.

MOON PIE
To celebrate the 40th anniversary of the first lunar landing, NASA created a giant moon pie in 2009. The special pie—consisting of marshmallow dipped in chocolate—measured 40 in (101 cm) in diameter, 6 in (15 cm) high, and weighed 55 lb (25 kg).

ELECTRIC PARADE
More than 200 electric vehicles formed a 2-mi-long (3-km) parade at Bay Harbor, Michigan, in 2009. The line was led by a Milburn Lite electric car dating back to 1920.

VARIED JOURNEY
Edwin Shackleton, an 82-year-old retired aircraft engineer from Bristol, England, traveled on 100 types of transport in just over six months. He started on New Year's Day 2009 with a car journey and racked up number 100 in July 2009 in a hot air balloon. On his way to his century, he traveled in such diverse modes of transport as a microlight, a fire truck, a garbage truck, a rickshaw, a police car, a chairlift, a quad bike, and a sled.

Giant Gummy

Derek Lawson makes giant gummy bears at Popalop's Candy Shop in Raleigh, North Carolina. Each one weighs a massive 5 lb (2 kg) and measures a whopping 9 x 5½ x 3½ in (23 x 14 x 9 cm), which is 1,400 times the size of an ordinary gummy bear. It takes nine hours to create each bear and make them taste exactly like the original smaller version. The bears are available in a variety of different flavors including blue raspberry, cola, grape, and green apple.

EXTRAORDINARY FEATS

WHOLE LOTTA SHAKIN'
In May 2009, Chris Raph of Minneapolis, Minnesota, bar manager at the Shout House Dueling Pianos bar, poured 662 cocktails in an hour, averaging over ten cocktails per minute.

ROBOT ACTORS
Robots appeared on stage alongside human actors in a play that premiered in Osaka, Japan, in 2008. The machines were specially programmed to speak lines with humans and move around the stage.

LATE FLIGHT
On May 6, 2009, Lillian Gardiner of St. Marys, Ontario, Canada, took her first ever plane ride—at the age of 105.

FROZEN FEAST
For the last 15 years of his life, eccentric U.S. movie producer Howard Hughes (1905–76) existed almost solely on a diet of ice cream. He usually ate the same flavor until every supplier in the district had run out.

CHOPSTICK CHALLENGE
In March 2009, Ashrita Furman of New York City ate 40 M&M's in a minute—with chopsticks.

BIRD STAMPS
Philatelist Daniel Monteiro of Mangalore, India, has a collection of nearly 5,000 postage stamps from over 260 countries—all featuring birds.

LIMBO SKATER
A five-year-old girl, Shreeya Rakesh Deshpande, from Maharashtra, India, limbo skated under a line of 27 parked cars—all just a few inches above the ground—covering a world record distance of 158 ft 2 in (48.2 m).

21 DEGREES
Professor Dr. Narayanam Narasimha Murthy of Nagpur, India, has acquired 29 degrees from 21 different universities and institutes around the world.

ZUMBA TEACHER
Catalina Mejia qualified as a Zumba instructor in December 2007 when she was just 11 years old. Now as a teenager she regularly runs classes at her local gym in Gaithersburg, Maryland.

PUZZLE QUEEN
Gina Lacuna holds the world's largest collection of jigsaw puzzles at her museum in Tagaytay, the Philippines. Among more than 470 puzzles, all of which she has completed single-handed, are some with over 18,000 pieces. Her first challenge was a 5,000-piece Mickey Mouse jigsaw bought for her son.

MODEL CARS
Dr. Hank Hammer of San Antonio, Texas, has a collection of over 36,000 model cars, built up since 1968. They are mostly Porsches, and his entire collection of 100,000 car-related items (including posters, books, and videos) is so big it is housed in two separate two-story homes.

R RAW BLOOD
A restaurant in Hanoi, Vietnam, serves customers a bowl of raw pig or duck blood at 75 cents each. Equally popular is a frozen pudding made from the fresh blood of the same animals.

R PRECISION WORK
Modern surgical robots move with such precision that they now have the ability to peel the skin from a grape.

R VALUABLE NOSE
Cheese tester Nigel Pooley from Somerset, England, has insured his nose for $8 million. He uses his refined sense of smell to select more than 12,000 tons of Cheddar cheese every year.

R LEPRECHAUN THRONG
In November 2011, 262 men, women, and children dressed as leprechauns gathered in Grand Canal Square, Dublin, Ireland.

R SMART BIKE
A bicycle designed to be as intelligent as a computer was unveiled by Britain's former Olympic champion racing cyclist Chris Boardman in 2009. The bike of the future could never be stolen and would feature puncture-proof, self-inflating tires, and a mini computer to count the calories as the pedals turned.

EYE-CATCHING
Yang Guanghe has a remarkable talent for using his eyelids to move heavy objects. In Guangzhou, China, in 2009, he dragged a car using ropes attached to his lower eyelids.

Daredevil Falls

Since 1901 a succession of "Niagara Daredevils" have made life-threatening attempts to conquer the rapid waters of the Canadian Horseshoe Falls, the highest drop at Niagara Falls, in various objects. Most seek fame, fortune, or publicity, some seek the thrill, and all of them are fully aware of the risk they take when they plunge over the top. The chances of survival are so slim that the jump is statistically more like suicide, with at least 12 to 15 suicides recorded at Niagara each year. Individuals who made early attempts were aptly named "daredevils" when they survived, with those that died being seen to have committed suicide. Although Niagara Falls are not the highest in the world, they are one of the most dangerous. The flow of water is so powerful that no man has ever been able to completely control it—not even trained engineers.

FORTUNE FALL – 1901
In October 1901, Annie Edison Taylor was the first person to drop down the Falls in a barrel—and survive. Annie was looking for some money and attention when she decided to conquer the falls at 63 years old (although she claimed to be in her forties). She emerged from the airtight wooden barrel with only a scratch on her forehead. Despite this, she never really became famous and spent the rest of her life selling souvenirs on the street.

A HEAD FOR HEIGHTS – 1886
The first man to conquer the Niagara Falls Rapids in a barrel was Carlisle Graham from Philadelphia. In July 1886, he took on the lower Great George Rapids through Lewiston, New York, in a 5½-ft (1.7-m) barrel made of oak and iron hoops, despite being about 6 ft (1.8 m) tall. The stunt took more than 30 minutes and, surviving the ride, he decided to do it again in August of the same year. This time he did it with his head hanging out of the top—the continuous force of the rapids on the side of his head damaged both his ear drums, leaving him deaf.

IN A SPIN – 1930
After helping Bobby Leach (see above) retrieve his barrel in 1911 and survive the fall, William Red Hill Sr. was in awe and decided to go over himself in 1930. He chose a 6 x 3 ft (2 x 1 m) steel barrel, with a 14 x 18 in (36 x 46 cm) manhole, and air holes that were secured with removable corks. More than 25,000 people watched him drop and within 90 seconds he was in the whirlpool at the bottom of the Falls where his barrel was trapped. After spinning for over three hours with his barrel half full of water, he finally emerged alive with only a few bruises.

www.ripleybooks.com

STEEL SQUEAL – 1911
In July 1911, Bobby Leach was the second person to take on the Falls in a barrel, but this one was made of steel. Leach was a performer with the Barnum & Bailey Circus and was sure he could complete the Falls even better than Annie had. The drop resulted in him breaking both his kneecaps and his jaw. However, he managed to use his experience to tour Canada, the United States, and New Zealand, telling people his story and posing with his barrel. He died later in life after contracting gangrene in his leg when he slipped on an orange peel.

BARREL OF NO RETURN – 1920
Charles G. Stephens was the first daredevil to lose his life going over the Horseshoe Falls in a barrel. On July 11, 1920, Englishman Stephens thought that he could save his 11 children from poverty and find fame by taking the plunge. Thousands watched as Stephens clambered into his large wooden barrel, tying his feet to an anvil for extra security. However, this turned out to be his fatal mistake, and when the barrel was recovered all that remained was his right arm.

INFLATABLE TALE – 1928
On July 4, 1928, Jean Lussier, a 36-year-old from Massachusetts, went over the Falls in an inflatable rubber ball 6 ft (1.8 m) in diameter. Although three of the 32 inner tubes burst, he survived.

HOW MUCH WATER?
The Canadian Horseshoe Falls is the highest drop of all at Niagara, descending 180 ft (55 m) and measuring 2,500 ft (760 m) across. However, the precise drop can vary by as much as 30 ft (9 m) depending on the season or even, sometimes, on the time of day. Around 45 million gallons (170 million liters) of water flows over the edge each minute—that's equivalent to about a million bathtubs of water tipping over the Falls every minute!

BALL OF FUN – 1961
In June 1961, Nathan Boya decided to attempt the Falls in a large ball. He declared that he was not seeking fame or fortune, but that it was "just something he had to do." He used a steel sphere wrapped in rubber that allowed him oxygen for 30 hours. After nearly dropping down the American Falls (the wrong one) and having to be towed back to the Horseshoe Falls, Nathan survived unscathed, yet incurred a $100 fine and $13 in court costs for illegally going over the Falls.

DOUBLE TROUBLE – 1989
In September 1989, two men took the plunge in the same barrel for the first time. Peter DeBernardi and Jeffrey Petkovich positioned themselves head to head wearing hockey helmets in a 10-x-5-ft (3-x-1.5-m) barrel. They emerged without serious injury.

JET JUMP – 1995
Robert Overacker, a 39-year-old school graduate, used a jet ski to drop over the Falls in October 1995. However, the rocket-propelled parachute strapped to his back failed to open and Robert fell 180 ft (55 m) to his death, a fall that is said to feel like hitting concrete.

WORTH THE WEIGHT – 1984
Canadian Karel Soucek went over the Falls in July 1984 in a lightweight wooden and plastic barrel, using a weight to ensure he went down feet first. His fall took about 3.2 seconds, going over at 75 mph (120 km/h). He suffered cuts and bruises, and an arm injury, as well as a $500 fine for stunting without a license!

DOUBLE DIVE – 1985 & 1993
Not content with going over the Falls once, Canadian Dave Munday did it twice! In 1985, Munday tumbled 173 ft (52.7 m) down Horseshoe Falls in five seconds in a 7-ft-long (2.1-m) steel barrel. In 1993, he did it again, in a diving bell. He had no helmet and there was just a 2-in (5-cm) layer of padding inside the bell to soften the impact.

GOING IT ALONE – 2003
In October 2003, Kirk Jones became the first daredevil to take on the Falls without any protection other than the clothes on his back. Climbing under the barrier, Kirk floated down the 175-ft (53-m) drop on his back and when he reached the bottom swam to some rocks. Refusing a helping hand from a *Maid of the Mist* tour boat, he climbed out to land on his own. He had only a couple of bruises, yet received a fine of $2,300 and was banned from Canada for life.

EXTRAORDINARY FEATS

Fast Fog

This amazing image captures the moment a U.S. Air Force B-2 Spirit Bomber created its own cloud as it approached the speed of sound near Los Angeles in 2009. Despite a wingspan of 172 ft (52 m), the bombers—which cost around $1 billion each when first made in 1989—are designed to be difficult to detect and can travel at 604 mph (972 km/h).

- The first plane to fly faster than the speed of sound was a Bell X-1 piloted by U.S. Air Force Captain Chuck Yeager, which reached a speed of 807 mph (1,299 km/h) in 1947.

- In 1979, Stan Barrett broke the sound barrier in a car. He achieved a speed of 739 mph (1,189 km/h) at Rogers Dry Lake, California, in his jet-powered Budweiser Rocket Car.

RIPLEY'S RESEARCH

The B-2 Spirit Bomber travels at such speed that a cloud of water vapor can form around its body. The phenomenon is often thought to be caused by the "sonic boom" heard when a plane travels faster than the speed of sound, but although the B-2 is incredibly quick, it falls short of the sound barrier. The cloud is probably caused by radical changes in air pressure when aircraft approach the speed of sound, which is about 760 mph (1,223 km/h) at sea level.

BABY BIKER
A three-year-old boy in India can ride a full-size motorcycle. Shantanu Khan from New Delhi extended the bike's controls so that son Azeem could reach them. Judges were so impressed they issued Azeem a special license to ride the bike around the neighborhood—but not on main roads.

ECONOMY SALAD
American Airlines saved an estimated $40,000 in 1987 by removing one olive from each salad served to first-class passengers.

FARMING FUNERAL
The coffin of farmer Gordon Hale from Wiltshire, England, was put on a trailer and towed to his grave by the Ford 4000 tractor he had used every day for 38 years. Maintaining the farming theme, mourners wore ribbons of bale twine, and the same material was used to form the handles on the coffin.

SOLAR FLIGHT
The Cardozo family from Wiltshire, England, traveled 1,242 mi (2,000 km) from Monte Carlo to Morocco in an electric paramotor (a motorized paraglider) powered by the sun. The paramotor was powered by lithium polymer batteries, which were charged in rotation using 12 solar panels on top of a support vehicle. Their journey across the Mediterranean took 15 days and they traveled at altitudes of up to 5,000 ft (1,500 m).

BIRTHDAY FLIGHTS
On his 16th birthday, Errick Smith of Ocean Springs, Mississippi, flew an airplane and a helicopter solo. Errick, who began taking flying lessons at 14, piloted a Cessna 172 aircraft and two helicopters, an R22, and a Schweitzer.

Flash Cars

English photographers Mark Brown and Marc Cameron have re-created the familiar shapes of well-known sports cars using only flashes of moving light and a camera. This vivid Bugatti Veyron is part of a collection inspired by various iconic cars, which also includes models from Ferrari, Morgan, and Aston Martin.

TITANIC TRIBUTE

In London, England, in February 2009, fans of the film *Titanic* donned Victorian costume and sat in old rowing boats as they watched a screening of the blockbuster movie in a swimming pool complete with dry ice and miniature icebergs. The real *Titanic* was an ocean liner that hit an iceberg and sank on its maiden voyage when crossing the Atlantic Ocean on April 14, 1912, with the loss of 1,517 lives.

When the *Titanic* hit an iceberg in 1912, the onboard cinema was showing an early silent film called *The Poseidon Adventure*, which by incredible coincidence tells the story of passengers escaping an ocean liner as it sinks to the bottom of the sea.

® DIRTY SEAT
Eighteen-year-old Jack Hyde from Oxfordshire, England, had his driver's test canceled in 2009 because the examiner found crumbs on his car seat.

® CHURCH AVOIDANCE
A seven-year-old boy trying to avoid going to church on a Sunday morning took his father's car for a drive around Plain City, Utah. Police officers chased the boy at speeds of 40 mph (65 km/h) before he stopped in a driveway.

® F1 LIMO
Canadian inventor Michael Pettipas has spent two years building a street-legal Formula-1 stretch limousine racing car with seven seats—six for passengers and one for the driver. The 30-ft-long (9-m) car has an 8-liter engine, can do 0 to 60 mph (0–97 km/h) in five seconds and is capable of reaching speeds of 140 mph (225 km/h).

® PET AIRWAYS
The maiden flight of an airline service that caters solely to pets took off from Farmingdale, New York, in July 2009. With Florida-based Pet Airways, founded by Alysa Binder and Dan Wiesel, pets travel in the airline's main cabin, but owners are not allowed onboard—even in the cargo hold. The company was founded in 2005 and the couple spent the next four years replacing seats with pet carriers in their fleet of five planes. Up to 50 animals at a time are escorted to the airplane by pet attendants, who give the animals a "potty break" just before takeoff and check on them every 15 minutes during the flight. At each of the five U.S. airports it serves, the company has even created a Pet Lounge for its animal passengers—or "pawsengers" as it calls them—where they can wait and sniff before flights.

® BIKE STAND
Mr. Liu, a farmer from Jiangxi, China, is able to stand, lie down, and even sleep on a motorcycle traveling at high speed. He once drove a motorbike for 3.7 mi (6 km) while standing.

® LOW MILEAGE
A Mini car that has been driven only 148 mi (238 km) was worth more in 2009 than it cost its owner in 1989. Ron Frost from Devon, England, paid about £5,800 for the 998cc cherry red Mini 30, but the longest journey it has ever made was 60 mi (96 km). For 20 years he has kept it indoors as part of his private car museum. Its oil has never been changed and it has been washed only twice. The British Mini Club says that the car, which is in pristine condition, would fetch up to £7,000 at auction.

® BOND FLYER
German Hermann Ramke has spent nine years developing a James Bond-like jet pack that is powered by high-pressure water. The JetLev-Flyer, which sells for around $140,000, has a top speed of 65 mph (105 km/h), can power the rider to an altitude of 33 ft (10 m), and is able to travel nearly 200 mi (320 km) before it needs refueling. A floating pump powered by a 150-hp four-stroke engine sends water through a 140-ft-long (43-m) hose to a pair of nozzles on the jet pack. The jet leaving the nozzles is powerful enough to propel the rider into the air.

EXTRAORDINARY FEATS

ORANGE MONEY
Chinese college student Wu Xiaobin paid for his 2009 course fees and living expenses with five tons of oranges. He drove two truckloads of mandarin oranges more than 130 mi (210 km) from the family farm in Quzhou to the city of Hangzhou, where he sold the fruit to fellow students so that he could continue his studies at Zhejiang University of Media and Communications.

HUGE FUDGE
In June 2009, Lansing Community College, Michigan, created a slab of chocolate fudge that weighed 5,500 lb (2,496 kg). The slab was made from 2,800 lb (1,270 kg) of chocolate, 705 lb (320 kg) of butter, and 305 gal (1,155 l) of condensed milk.

UNDERSEA MAIL
In 2009, a Norwegian mayor sent a letter to an English town through a 725-mi (1,166-km) underwater gas pipeline running beneath the North Sea. Bernard Riksfjord, mayor of Aukra in western Norway, dropped the letter into the Langeled pipeline on August 19, 2009, and five days later the letter, propelled forward by pressurized gas, popped out in the town of Easington, County Durham.

WARNING SUIT
To make people aware of the threat of skin cancer, a Canadian company has designed a two-piece bathing suit that changes color to warn women when the sun's rays are too strong. The bikini is held together with pale decorative beads that turn dark purple if the UV rays reach dangerous levels.

CHAMP CHESTNUT
Joey Chestnut of San Jose, California, swallowed 68 hot dogs in ten minutes to capture his third straight Fourth of July hot-dog eating contest at Coney Island in 2009. His winning technique is to grab two hot dogs at a time, force them into his mouth and, with a minimal number of chews, gulp them down. He then dips the buns in water and simply lets them slide down his throat.

EPIC VOYAGE
Although paralyzed from the neck down, 37-year-old Hilary Lister from Kent, England, sailed solo around the U.K. in 2009—a distance of 1,500 mi (2,415 km). She operated the 20-ft (6-m) racing yacht by blowing through straws connected to a computer. Her epic voyage took her three months and she covered approximately 60 mi (96 km) a day. Wheelchair-bound since the age of 15, Hilary, who suffers from Reflex Sympathetic Dystrophy, earned a degree in biochemistry at Oxford University despite having to dictate her papers with an epidural drip in her spine.

PASTA BOWL
In March 2009, a restaurant in Doha, Qatar, dished up a bowl of pasta measuring 20 ft (6 m) long and 6 ft 6 in (2 m) wide, and weighing 9,480 lb (4,300 kg).

Pear of Buddhas

After more than six years of work, Gao Xianzhang from Hebei, China, has managed to modify a crop of pears to look like little Buddhas. In 2009, after a lot of effort and rotten fruit, he perfected a technique and was able to mold 10,000 pears into edible Buddha-shaped fruit. Selling them for $10 each, the pears, which resemble baby Buddhas, are grown in special plastic molds on the tree branches from an early stage.

Life in the Skies

To conquer his phobia of flying, Mark Malkoff from New York spent an entire month on an airplane in June 2009. Traveling up to 12 flights a day and 135 in total, he touched down at 38 U.S. airports, spent 267 hours in the air, and covered a distance of 111,972 mi (180,201 km) or 4.5 times the circumference of the Earth. Under the rules of the challenge, he was forbidden from actually setting foot in any airport and so had to rest on the plane wings or take a shower on the runway courtesy of a fire truck!

Ripley's ask

Did you eat airplane food all month?
I ate some airplane food. Most of the food was airport food that was brought to me by my crew or people who felt sorry for me. Sometimes I'd go on Twitter and ask for food, which worked very well.

How did you wash?
The plane of course didn't have a shower, so every morning I washed with baby wipes. I washed my hair over the airplane bathroom sink. One time a flight attendant shampooed my hair mid-flight.

Where did you sleep?
I slept alone on the plane in a different row every night. The plane was completely empty. I had my own pillow and sleeping bag. Most nights the cleaning crew had to vacuum around me as I slept.

Did you get bored?
I was never bored. I was constantly meeting people, filming videos, and during flights was keeping in touch with people using Gogo wi-fi.

And finally... did you get over your fear of flying?
After about a week I slowly started to get over my fear of flying by talking to pilots. They really helped me to understand turbulence, which was a huge fear of mine.

RODE KILL

Californian hot-rod artist John Towers has created "Rode Kill," a unique, handcrafted, custom motorcycle seemingly made from a decaying corpse. The bike has incredibly detailed features such as a heart protruding from an exposed ribcage that houses the fuel tank, and super-realistic bones that flex at the elbow with the bike suspension.

Look closer and you will see maggots crawling over the decaying flesh, bloodstained exhaust pipes, and headlight eyes in the skull. John wanted to graphically drive home how dangerous powerful motorbikes can be for inexperienced riders— "Rode Kill" will reach speeds of 140 mph (225 km/h).

Maggots!

www.ripleybooks.com

EXTRAORDINARY FEATS

R GAMING MARATHON
Brett Carow of Farmington, Minnesota, and Sam Hennemann of Minneapolis, Minnesota, played the board game Strat-O-Matic Baseball for 61 hours 2 minutes at a New York City bar, setting a new world record for marathon gaming. In that time they played over 100 games and rolled the dice about 10,000 times.

R MISSING PIECE
Gretha Glasel of Norfolk, England, spent six months assembling the world's largest jigsaw puzzle—a 32,256-piece monster measuring 17 x 6 ft (5.2 m x 1.8 m)—only to find that a piece was missing. She was only able to finish it by ordering the last piece from the manufacturers.

R WORLD KNOWLEDGE
At just two years old, Sherwyn Sarabi of South Yorkshire, England, could name every country in the world. He could identify all 195 independent sovereign states on a map of the world and even match them with their national flags.

R LIGHTNING REFLEXES
Anthony Kelly, from Armidale, New South Wales, Australia, has incredibly fast reflexes even when he is unable to see. On separate occasions, he has caught 904 tennis balls in an hour, 43 tennis balls in a minute, and 11 tennis balls in a minute, the last time while blindfolded. On each occasion the balls were fired at him from just 20 ft (6 m) at speeds in excess of 62.5 mph (100 km/h).

R ANGEL'S FAN
A dedicated fan of the TV series Charlie's Angels, Jack Condon of Sherman Oaks, California, has more than 5,500 items of memorabilia related to the show. He began his collection in 1976 when the show debuted and even drives around in the original pink Charlie's Angels van. In total, he has more than 15,000 press cuttings, 7,000 photographs, and 500 magazines featuring the various Angels actresses throughout their careers.

R ARROW CATCHER
Californian Tyler Burke caught eight arrows with his hand in two minutes while blindfolded, doubling the previous world record. The arrows were fired by his brother Brandon.

R YOGA TEACHER
Ida Herbert of Toronto, Ontario, still teaches yoga at age 98, making her the world's oldest yoga teacher. She has been practicing yoga since the late 1940s and gets up at 5.30am most days to perform her poses.

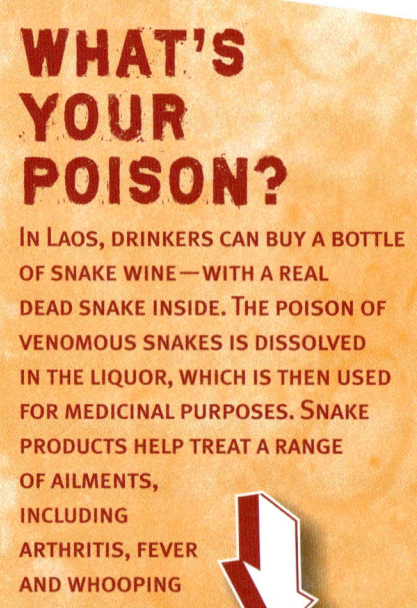

WHAT'S YOUR POISON?
IN LAOS, DRINKERS CAN BUY A BOTTLE OF SNAKE WINE—WITH A REAL DEAD SNAKE INSIDE. THE POISON OF VENOMOUS SNAKES IS DISSOLVED IN THE LIQUOR, WHICH IS THEN USED FOR MEDICINAL PURPOSES. SNAKE PRODUCTS HELP TREAT A RANGE OF AILMENTS, INCLUDING ARTHRITIS, FEVER AND WHOOPING COUGH.

Hopping Mad

Pan-fried grasshopper is considered a delicacy in Korea and other parts of Asia. Insect gourmets say it tastes best seasoned with lime or salt, or dipped in garlic butter.

SANDOW

Eugene Sandow, real name Friedrich Muller, was born in 1867 in Konigsberg, Prussia. He was the first popular male strongman. Performing mostly in circuses and sideshows, he was famous for his bulging muscles and for breaking chains around his chest until his death in 1925. He notoriously wore a skimpy costume.

HANDSTAND

Robert Jones from Pine Bluff, Arkansas, become famous for this incredible stunt—a handstand while balancing on two juggling clubs. On his 50th birthday he managed to cut his birthday cake with one hand while performing a one-handed handstand on the table with the other.

SANDWINA

Sandwina was known as "The Strongest and Most Beautiful Woman in the World." She would bend rods and straighten horseshoes to the delight of large audiences who saw her perform with the Ringling Bros. and Barnum & Bailey Circus in the early 20th century. She was born Katie Brumbach, one of 14 children, and performed with her parents Philippe and Johanna Brumbach. Her father would offer 100 marks to any man who could defeat her in wrestling—no one ever won the prize! Sandwina defeated the strongman Eugene Sandow (left) by lifting a 300-lb (135-kg) weight over her head—Sandow only managed to lift it to his chest. It was after beating the strong man that Katie adopted her stage name, "Sandwina."

Strong Tongue

Habu, known as the "Man with the Iron Tongue," was a 1930s strongman from India who was able to lift up to 105 lb (48 kg) by hooking the weight to his tongue and lifting it from above.

Knuckle Duster

Mick Gooch must have the strongest fingers in the world. The martial arts expert from Kent, England, is capable of 17 one-armed, single-finger push-ups on the head of a nail. Mick was inspired by the two-finger push-ups performed by kung-fu legend Bruce Lee, and decided to go one incredible step further, a feat that took years of dedication—and broken knuckles—to master.

EXTRAORDINARY FEATS

℞ HISTORIC FLIGHT
In 2009, to mark the centenary of French inventor and pilot Louis Blériot becoming the first person to fly an airplane across the English Channel, another Frenchman, Edmond Salis, repeated the 22-mi (35-km) crossing in a restored Blériot XI—the same model used by his predecessor on that 1909 flight.

℞ PASSENGER PILOT
Passenger Doug White took over the controls and landed a twin engine plane at Southwest Florida International Airport in April 2009—after the pilot died in mid-flight.

℞ BUSY AIRPORT
The Hartsfield–Jackson International Airport in Atlanta, Georgia, serves 90 million passengers a year—more than the entire population of Germany.

℞ CAMEL CHOCS
Dubai-based company Al Nassma specializes in making camel-milk chocolates. It has 3,000 camels, which produce enough milk to make 100 tons of low-fat chocolate.

℞ PRESERVED WRECK
The HMS *Ontario*, a British warship that sank in Lake Ontario off the coast of New York State, was discovered in 2008 in excellent condition, despite being underwater for 228 years.

℞ FLIGHT RAPPER
U.S. flight attendant David Holmes got so bored with reading out the safety instructions that he decided to rap them. His 80-second rap included: "Before we leave, our advice is, put away your electronic devices. Fasten your seat belt, then put your trays up—press the button and make the seat belt raise up."

℞ HAIR-RAISING
Over 30,000 women and more than 100 long-haired men from Myanmar donated their hair to pay for repairs to a road leading to the remote Buddhist pagoda of Alaungdaw Kathapha. Nearly 1,750 lb (800 kg) of hair was collected, with some locks measuring up to 4 ft (1.2 m) long. The hair was then sold to traders in China for use in wigs or dolls, while the money raised improved access on the pagoda road.

Car Crash
Visitors to a square in Berlin, Germany, had to look twice when they encountered a car that appeared to have fallen from the sky and smashed through the pavement. It was actually a convincing sculpture conceived as a publicity stunt by a German website.

At temperatures of –58°F (–50°C), if a truck falls through the ice and sinks into the water, the driver has less than one minute to get out before freezing to death.

The ice needs to be 40 in (102 cm) thick to withstand the largest 70-ton trucks. Speeds on the frozen road are often limited to below 20 mph (32 km/h) to minimize potential damage as the ice shifts.

Every winter, hundreds of truckers risk their lives by driving monster 18-wheeled rigs weighing over 50 tons across frozen lakes and rivers, and even the frozen Arctic Sea. The ice-road truckers make as many runs as possible (the "dash for cash" as they call it), each run taking over 20 hours. Driving hundreds of miles at a time, over sheets of ice just 28 in (70 cm) thick, truckers drive on little sleep and are in constant fear of the sound of cracking ice beneath their wheels, a sound that could send them plunging to their death.

RIPLEY'S RESEARCH

The ice-road truckers deliver vital supplies to diamond mines and gas plants in Canada's remote Northwest Territories. These ice roads stretch for over 1,550 mi (2,500 km) and are accessible for only 60 days a year before they start to melt. At the start of each season, a profiler vehicle is sent out to test the thickness of the ice with a radar. Once the road is declared safe, plows take to the ice to clear away the snow.

DRIVING ON THIN ICE

INDEX

Page numbers in *italics* refer to illustrations

A
actors, robotic 18
airplanes
 airline for pets 23
 bomber creates cloud 22, *22*
 breaking sound barrier 22, *22*
 first flight across English Channel 32
 first flight for centenarian 18
 flight to wrong destination 11
 flying cars 11
 living on for a month 25, *25*
 passenger repairs 8
 pilot dies 32
 pulling 12, *12*
 safety instructions rapped 32
 very young pilot 22
 weight-saving tactic 22
airport, very busy 32
aluminum, transparent form of 13
Amazon River, walking length of 6, *7*
arrows, catching in hand 28
astronauts, odorless underwear for 12
Australia, driving to 8

B
balls, blind man catches 28
Barrett, Stan (U.S.A.) 22
baseball
 fans eat potato chips 8
 marathon board game session 28
Basso, Kevin (U.S.A.) 9, *9*
Bertoletti, Pat "Deep Dish" (U.S.A.) 8
bicycles
 cycling through many countries 11
 very fast 13
 very intelligent 19
bikini, skin cancer warning 24
Binder, Alysa (U.S.A.) 23
birds
 pigeon faster than Internet 12
 on postage stamps 18
Bleriot, Louis (Fra) 32
blind man, catches tennis balls 28
blindfolded, catching arrows 28
Block, Ken (U.S.A.) 10, *10*
blood, restaurant serves 19
board game, marathon session 28
Boardman, Chris (U.K.) 19
boats and ships
 large collection of model ships 8
 paralyzed woman sails 24
 underwater boat 11, *11*
 watching *Titanic* movie in 23, *23*
 wreck of warship found 32
Boya, Nathan (U.S.A.) 21, *21*
Brown, Mark (U.K.) 22, *22*
Brumbach, Philippe and Johanna (U.S.A.) 31
Buddha, pears look like 24
bullets, handkerchief stops 13
Burke, Tyler and Brandon (U.S.A.) 28
Burnett, Charles III (U.S.A.) 11
bus, driver has heart attack 11

C
camel-milk chocolates 32
Cameron, Marc (U.K.) 22, *22*
cancer, bikini warns of risk 24
Cardozo family (U.K.) 22
Carow, Brett (U.S.A.) 28
cars
 breaks sound barrier 22
 burial in 11
 crumbs cause driving test failure 23
 dragging with eyelids *18–19*, 19
 early snowmobile 15, *15*
 extreme driving on snow 10, *10*
 flying 11
 limbo skating under 18
 made with moving light 22, *22*
 sculpture of car crash 32, *32*
 steam-powered 11
 stretch limousine racing car 23
 trapped in mudflats 11
 very large collection of model cars 18
 very low mileage 23
 very young boy drives 23
cats, airline for pets 23
centenarians
 eats large quantities of chocolate 16
 first plane ride for 18
 paragliding 13
chandelier, made of gummy bears 16, *16*
Charlie's Angels, very large collection of memorabilia 28
cheese
 perfect sandwich 16
 tester insures nose 19
chefs, robot 8
Chestnut, Joey (U.S.A.) 24
chicken nugget, giant 16
chocolate
 camel-milk chocolates 32
 centenarian eats large quantities of 16
 enormous slab of fudge 24
chopsticks, eating M&Ms with 18
Chou, Ya Ya (U.S.A.) 16, *16*
cloud, bomber creates 22, *22*
cocktails, pouring multiple 18
coffee, taster insures tongue 16
coffin, towed to funeral by tractor 22
computer, very powerful 13
Condon, Jack (U.S.A.) 28
Conti, "Crazy Legs" (U.S.A.) 9
corpse, motorcycle looks like 26, *26–7*
countries, small child identifies on map 28
cremation ashes, buried in car 11

D
dance, very young Zumba instructor 18
DeBernardi, Peter (U.S.A.) 21, *21*
Deshpande, Shreeya Rakesh (Ind) 18
dinosaurs, prehistoric-themed restaurant 8
dogs, airline for pets 23

E
ears, lifting weights with 13, *13*
electric vehicles, very long parade of 16
English Channel, first flight across 32
eyelids, dragging car with *18–19*, 19

F
Fast, Rev. Kevin (Can) 12, *12*
Fernandez, Ramon (U.S.A.) 11
fingers, push-ups on one 30, *31*
flags, small child identifies 28
flight
 first flight across English Channel 32
 first flight for centenarian 18
 flying cars 11
 water-powered jet pack 23
food, speed eating 8, 9, *9*, 24
Frost, Ron (U.K.) 23
fudge, enormous slab of 24
funeral, coffin towed by tractor 22
Furman, Ashrita (U.S.A.) 18
Furze, Colin (U.K.) 11

G
Gao Xianzhang (Chn) 24, *24*
Gardiner, Lillian (Can) 18
gas pipeline, letter sent through 24
Gernsback, Hugo 15, *15*
Glasel, Gretha (U.K.) 28
glasses, television 15, *15*
Gooch, Mick (U.K.) 30, *31*
Graham, Carlisle (U.S.A.) 20, *20*
grasshoppers, eating 29, *29*
Griffiths, Peggy (U.K.) 16
gummy bears
 chandelier made of 16, *16*
 giant 17, *17*
gun, shooting round corners 14, *14*
Guzy, Rachel (U.S.A.) 11

H
Habu (Ind) 31, *31*
hair, pays for road repairs 32
Hale, Gordon (U.K.) 22
Hammer, Dr. Hank (U.S.A.) 18
handkerchief, stops bullets 13
hands
 catching arrows 28
 handstand on juggling clubs 30, *30*
 push-ups on one finger 30, *31*
Hart, Terry (U.K.) 11
helicopters
 very old 14, *14*
 very young pilot 22
Hennemann, Sam (U.S.A.) 28
Herbert, Ida (Can) 28
Hill, William Red Sr. (U.S.A.) 20
Holmes, David (U.S.A.) 32
Horgmo, Torstein 10
Horseshoe Falls 20–1, *20–1*
hot dogs
 giant 8
 speed eating 24
Hughes, Howard (U.S.A.) 18
Hyde, Jack (U.K.) 23

I
ice, driving trucks on 33, *33*
ice cream, living on 18
insects, eating grasshoppers 29, *29*
International Space Station 12
Internet, pigeon faster than 12
Iwasaki, Keiichi (Jap) 11

J
jet pack, water-powered 23
jigsaw puzzles
 enormous 28
 very large collection of 18

Jones, Kirk (U.S.A.) 21
Jones, Robert (U.S.A.) 30, *30*

K
Kelly, Anthony (Aus) 28
Khan, Shantanu and Azeem (Ind) 22
kibbeh, giant 8
Kolos, Farkas (Hun) 11

L
Lacuna, Gina (Phi) 18
lakes, driving trucks on frozen 33, *33*
Lawson, Derek (U.S.A.) 17, *17*
Leach, Bobby (U.S.A.) 20–1, *20*
Lee, Bruce (U.S.A.) 31
leprechauns, mass gathering dressed as 19
limbo skating, under cars 18
Lister, Hilary (U.K.) 24
Liu, Mr. (Chn) 23
Lussier, Jean (U.S.A.) 21, *21*

M
M&M's, eating with chopsticks 18
McAlpine, Peggy (U.K.) 13
mail, sent through gas pipeline 24
Malkoff, Mark (U.S.A.) 25, *25*
Mejia, Catalina (U.S.A.) 18
milk, camel-milk chocolates 32
Monteiro, Daniel (Ind) 18
moon pie, enormous 16
motorcycles
    child rides 22
    enormous jump on 13
    looks like a corpse 26, *26–7*
    sleeping on 23
    very long 11
movies, watching *Titanic* in boats 23, *23*
Moyen, Branden (U.S.A.) 13
mud, car trapped in 11
Munday, Dave (Can) 21
Murthy, Dr. Narayanam Narasimha (Ind) 18

N
Naismith, Graham and Eirene (U.K.) 8
navel, lint in 13
Niagara Falls, going over in a barrel 20–1, *20–1*
nose, cheese tester insures 19

O
oranges, college course paid for with 24
Overacker, Robert (U.S.A.) 21

P
paragliding
    by centenarian 13
    powered by sun 22
pasta, restaurant serves giant bowl of 24
pears, look like Buddhas 24, *24*
Pelliccia, Gennaro (Ita) 16
Pescara, Raul (Spa) 14, *14*
Petkovich, Jeffrey (U.S.A.) 21, *21*
Pettipas, Michael (Can) 23
pigeon, faster than Internet 12
pipeline, letter sent through 24
poison, snake wine 28, *28–9*
Pooley, Nigel (U.K.) 19
postage stamps, very large collection of 18
potato chips, baseball fans eat 8
push-ups, on one finger 30, 31

R
Ramke, Hermann (Ger) 23
Raph, Chris (U.S.A.) 18
rapping, airplane safety instructions 32
Recht, Sruli (Ice) 13
Renner, Ronnie (U.S.A.) 13
restaurants
    eating with dinosaurs 8
    giant bowl of pasta 24
    giant chicken nugget 16
    robot chefs 8
    serves blood 19
ribs, speed eating 8
Riksfjord, Bernard (Nor) 24
Rinfret, John H.T. (U.S.A.) 14
Ringling Bros. and Barnum & Baily Circus 31
rivers
    driving trucks on frozen 33, *33*
    walking length of Amazon 6, *7*
roads
    hair pays for repairs 32
    ice roads 33, *33*
robberies, anti-bandit bag 14
robots
    actors 18
    chefs 8
    surgeons 19
roller coaster, large model of 13
Rutten, Joannes (Nld) 11

S
sailor, paralyzed 24
Salis, Edmond (Fra) 32
Sandow, Eugene 30, *30*, 31
sandwich, perfect cheese 16
Sandwina (U.S.A.) 31, *31*
Sarabi, Sherwyn (U.K.) 28
sculpture, of car crash 32, *32*
Shackleton, Edwin (U.K.) 16
Sharma, Rakesh (Ind) 13, *13*
ships *see* boats and ships
skating, limbo skating under cars 18
sleep, on motorcycle 23
Smith, Errick (U.S.A.) 22
snakes, dead snake in bottles of wine 28, *28–9*
snow
    early snowmobile 15, *15*
    extreme driving on 10, *10*
Soucek, Karel (Can) 21
Stafford, Ed (U.K.) 6, *7*
steam-powered car 11
Steinhauser, Dr. Georg (Aut) 13
Stephens, Charles G. (U.K.) 21, *21*
Stephenson, George (U.K.) 11
strong men and women 30–1, *30–1*
    dragging car with eyelids 18–19, *19*
    lifting weights with ears 13, *13*
    pulling airplane 12, *12*
    push-ups on one finger 30, 31
sun bathing, bikini warns of cancer risk 24
surgery, by robots 19
Swanson, George (U.S.A.) 11

T
Tamm, Peter (Ger) 8
Taylor, Annie Edison (U.S.A.) 20, *20*
Taylor, Moulton (U.S.A.) 11
television
    television glasses 15, *15*
    very large collection of Charlie's Angels memorabilia 28
Titanic, watching movie in boats 23, *23*
tomato fight 8, *8*
tongue
    coffee taster insures 16
    lifting weights with 31, *31*
Towers, John (U.S.A.) 26, *26–7*
tractor, tows coffin to funeral 22
trains
    effects of speed on passengers 11
    track stolen 11
transport, traveling on multiple types of 16
trucks, driving on ice 33, *33*

U
underwater boat 11, *11*
underwear, odorless for astronauts 12
universities
    multiple degrees from 18
    student pays for college course with oranges 24

W
Wakata, Koichi (Jap) 12
waterfalls, going over Niagara Falls in barrels 20–1, *20–1*
weights
    dragging car with eyelids 18–19, *19*
    lifting with ears 13, *13*
    lifting with tongue 31, *31*
    pulling airplane 12, *12*
White, Doug (U.S.A.) 32
Whittingham, Sam (Can) 13
Wiesel, Dan (U.S.A.) 23
wine, dead snakes in bottles of 28, *28–9*
Wu Xiaobin (Chn) 24

Y
yacht, paralyzed woman sails 24
Yang Guanghe (Chn) 18–19, *19*
Yeager, Chuck (U.S.A.) 22
yoga, elderly teacher 28

Z
Zumba, very young instructor 18

ACKNOWLEDGMENTS

COVER (t) Concept, design, sculpture by John Towers of Blue Flame Alley Studios, Florida/Photos courtesy of Horst Rösler, Germany/Special thanks for Kate Towers for her endless support, (c) Scubacraft 2010, (b) Johnny McCormack; 4 Scubacraft 2010; 6 (b/r) © Julien Scaperrotta—Fotolia.com, (t/l) © Roberto—Fotolia.com, (l) © Stefanie Leuker—Fotolia.com; 6–7 (dp) Photo's by Keith Ducatel www.keithducatel.com; 8–9 Getty Images; 10 Johnny McCormack; 11 Scubacraft 2010; 12 Bill Tremblay/The Independent; 13 Simon De Trey-White/Barcroft Media Ltd; 14 (l, c) Getty Images, (r) © Photoshot; 15 (l) AP/Press Association Images, (r) Time & Life Pictures/Getty Images; 16 YaYa Chou; 17 Vat19.com; 19 ChinaFotoPress/Photocome/Press Association Images; 20 (l, b/c, t/r) Niagara Falls (Ontario) Public Library, (c/r) © Bettmann/Corbis; 20–21 (dp) © Filtv—Fotolia.com; 21 (t/l, b/l, b/c) Niagara Falls (Ontario) Public Library; 22 (t) Rex Features, (b) Marc Cameron/Mark Brown/Rex Features; 23 Chris Jackson/Getty Images; 24 Wenn.com; 25 Mark Malkoff; 26–27 Concept, design, sculpture by John Towers of Blue Flame Alley Studios, Florida/Photos courtesy of Horst Rösler, Germany/Special thanks for Kate Towers for her endless support; 29 (t) Reuters/Natalie Behring; 30 (l) Time & Life Pictures/Getty Images; (b) Chatham News; 31 (b) Getty Images; BACK COVER Vat19.com

Key: t = top, b = bottom, c = center, l = left, r = right, sp = single page, dp = double page

All other photos are from Ripley Entertainment Inc.
Every attempt has been made to acknowledge correctly and contact copyright holders and we apologize in advance for any unintentional errors or omissions, which will be corrected in future editions.